Gingerboy's Search for Christmas

by
Joanne Kimberly

Illustrated by John Babcock

Gingerboy's Search for Christmas

I dedicate this book to my husband, David. He is the love of my life, the joy of my heart, and my best friend. Every time I hear his car pull in the driveway, I get just as excited as I did the first day we met.

I also dedicate this book to the three most precious gifts the Lord chose to give me—my children: James, Cindy, and TJ. Each one is such a unique treasure, my heart abounds with delight and love whenever I am with them. I marvel that the Lord could love them more than I do, and yet I know He does.

And to my daughter-in-law Alaina and my son-in-law Danny who have added even more laughter and love to our home. I cherish the day they each became a part of our family.

And finally, to my granddaughter Aislynn, who is sugar and spice and everything amazing! It is such fun loving you!

Joanne Kimberly
c/o Happy Place Books LLC
PO Box 291
Massillon, OH 44648
joanne@happyplacebooks.com

Fourth Edition: 2017

Printed in the United States of America

ISBN: 978-0-9904893-4-4

CHAPTER 1

He wasn't quite sure
when he first came alive—
was it perhaps when the Baker
gently put in his eyes?

Or the time when the Baker
first smiled down at him,
and he used his new mouth
to give back his first grin.

Or was it when the Baker
spoke with great authority,
saying, "Rise, Gingerboy!
Be all you can be!"

Or maybe when the Baker
gave Gingerboy a hug,
and his heart started beating,
and he knew he was loved.

1

Every day after that first day,
together became the plan;
the Baker even naming
Gingerboy his right-hand man.

Gingerboy would stir the batter,
put the brownies in to bake,
roll the dough to make the donuts,
and paint frosting on each cake.

When the day of work had ended,
they would lick a spoon or two—
Gingerboy, the brownie batter,
and the Baker, chocolate mousse.

Of course, they had their break time
waiting for the bread to rise,
when they often played a board game
while they snacked on apple pie.

King me, Mr. Baker!

But the greatest joy for Gingerboy
was to hear the Baker say,
"Well done, my little helper,
you have served me well today."

With the daylight disappearing
and the nighttime rushing in—
dinner done, the fire burning—
story time would soon begin.

Gingerboy put on his jammies
then raced for the sofa chair.
Two large arms were sure to catch him,
and he found great comfort there.

Gingerboy was quite surprised
when no storybook was there!
Could it be bedtime already?
Or a book hidden somewhere?

"Where are the books, Mr. Baker?
Don't you know it's story time?"
The Baker gave a chuckle.
"I had something else in mind."

Gingerboy's eyes searched the room.
"Is there a present here somewhere?"
"If there is, I think you'll find it
underneath my sofa chair."

No books?

Bedtime
so soon?

Like a bat hung upside-down,
that is how the boy behaved.
The Baker gripped each ginger leg
as he searched inside the "*cave*."

"I found it!" his voice echoed.
"Pull me out!" he then exclaimed.
As his body came into the light,
he brought out a large black train.

Gingerboy had never seen one,
except in the books they'd read.
Every page brought trains to life.
"Toot-toot, chugga-chugga," he said.

What delight the Baker felt
watching Gingerboy at play.
But he had another reason
for the gift he gave that day.

A train!

Thank you!

Back up in the Baker's arms,
Gingerboy gave a tender kiss.
He always loved his presents,
but none of them compared to this.

The Baker sadly knew
for Gingerboy the time was near
when, in the search for more,
he would lose what was most dear.

His journey would be hard,
but he'd find help along the way,
and this train that he adored
would mean much more to him someday.

Another son the Baker loved
had come to earth to heal
and give back to Gingerboy
what evil tried to steal.

Looking at his Gingerboy,
the Baker gave him a gentle squeeze.
What he'd say might be confusing;
he hoped Gingerboy would believe.

"My dear boy, I have a son,
I've loved before time ever started.
I've sent him to save the world
and to heal the broken-hearted."

Gingerboy asked, "After he saves the world, will he come to be with you once more?"
The Baker reached over and gave him a kiss.
"Yes, and pain will be gone forevermore."

Then Gingerboy wondered, "Would it be all right,
since your son has left and gone away,
if I were your son for just a little while?
I'd have a family and Papa that way."

The Baker's big laugh then filled up the room,
and his hug filled Gingerboy's heart.
"I love you, my son, and your Papa I am.
I delight in all that you are."

Gingerboy jumped on his Papa's back
in the usual piggy-back style.
Tonight's ride to bed would be on a train.
"All aboard," Papa said with a smile.

"Chugga-chugga, toot-toot." They were fast on their way,
'til Papa's foot jammed on the brake.
"We've arrived at your stop here in Sleepy-Time Land.
Off to bed now. It's getting quite late!"

Gingerboy demanded not one hug, but two.
"I love you, my Papa! You know that I do."
"But I love you more," Papa said with a smile.
Gingerboy knew it would always be true.

Chugga chugga
toot-toot!

CHAPTER 2

When he woke the next morning, Gingerboy had a plan—
a day full of cool winter fun.
He would build a large fort and a hefty snowman
and maybe go on a toboggan run.

Gingerboy skipped his breakfast,
put a hat on his head.
He'd have the snowman done
before Papa rolled out of bed.

As he stepped out the door,
he rubbed and blinked both his eyes.
Standing one jump away on the gate's other side
stood a bustling fair 'neath a warm summer sky.

One booth sold hot muffins, another fresh bread.
In the center, the fruit pies were made.
His eyes followed the stairs to a large central tower
where there were cakes and fried donuts displayed.

There were wolves there to serve, of the most friendly kind,
making sure customers were always right.
Down a wide road they came—herds of bleating sheep-shoppers,
herds and herds with no shepherd in sight.

Where did this
come from?

Gingerboy was spellbound by the summertime scene
and drawn in by the sweet treats' aroma.
One wolf welcomed him to join in the fun
with an overly friendly persona.

The wolf was so tall, his red chef hat stood high,
in his hand he held a devil's-food cake.
Chocolate was Gingerboy's greatest love;
he was finding it a struggle to wait.

Gingerboy asked, "Chocolate chips on the top?"
The wolf grinned. "Yes! One piece or two?"
"I so want a bite, but I have no money."
"It's on the house! I only want YOU!"

The next moment an angry Papa was there.
The wolf made a quick dash to hide.
The towering festival slipped into the sun.
Gingerboy felt his own anger inside.

Later that night Papa tucked him in bed
as he wrestled with so many thoughts.
"I wanted the cake, but with you standing there,
what I started to do, I did not."

"Please tell me Papa, 'cause I don't understand.
Why did you get angry today?
All I wanted to taste was a piece of that cake.
When you showed up, you got in the way."

"The wolf's trying, my son, to take you from me
to his dark world of lies and deceit.
He used the temptation he knew you'd love most—
cakes and goodies so sugary sweet."

"He had to make sure his trap would do the trick—
like a fair in the warm summer sun.
But my dear Gingerboy, what you saw wasn't true,
and it wasn't created for fun!"

"He's waiting right now, hoping you'll make the choice
to sample each delicious treat.
But the moment you're eating right out of his hand,
you'll find you've had too much to eat."

"What once tasted good will make you quite sick.
You will ask for a bed and a hug.
And the wolf dressed in red will just laugh at your pain;
he only wants to destroy whom I love."

Why, Papa?

Gingerboy didn't answer. He couldn't believe that his Papa would lie to him now.
'Cause the wolf seemed so friendly and the treats looked so good;
Papa must be mistaken somehow.

"Don't I have the free will to sample the sweets
and make the choice to disobey?
If it's not what you like, but it is what I want,
now and then it should just be okay."

His Papa looked sad as he spoke to his son.
He knew they were drifting apart.
"The rules that I give aren't to rob you of joy,
but to keep you safe here in my heart."

"When you're happy, I'm happy. I seek only your joy,
and to save you from what sin can do.
If you love me, then you'll want to follow my rules,
for love must be a choice to be true."

Gingerboy could not quiet his mind—
devil's food cake and chocolate cream pie.
He dreamed of huge cakes with more custard inside
and clouds of whipped cream in the sky.

yum

yum

The sun ended his struggle; he would have what he wanted.
He would taste every treat at the fair.
Tip-toeing 'cross the kitchen; no need for a coat—
"It will feel just like summer out there."

As he closed the back door, a cold wind made him shiver.
The doubts in his mind he quick pushed away.
"I'm not scared," he declared. "I'll be home before dinner."
He stepped out; he was getting his way.

At the gate, he touched the latch,
to the other side he crossed.
The fair then quickly vanished;
in a moment, all was lost!

Angry wolves gathered 'round him,
his whole body shook with fear.
He cried out for his Papa,
but the wolves - all he could hear.

In the center of the circle,
stood the leader of the pack.
One signal from this fierce wolf
and the others would attack.

The **same wolf** without his chef hat!
But not friendly now, not kind!
No more cakes or pies he offered,
only evil on his mind.

It's YOU!

The wolf was having such a good time,
and he wanted it to last.
"I'll give you a running start, boy,
but you'd better make it fast!"

Gingerboy turned and fled,
wanting only to survive.
"Papa!" he screamed out.
"Please help me stay alive!"

The head wolf began to chuckle,
as the others watched the show—
the boy running for his life now.
Then their leader sneered, "Let's go."

Gingerboy's teeth were chattering.
He couldn't see through all his tears.
Every inch of him was trembling.
He had never known such fear.

PAPA!

Save me!

The wind beat at his body.
He had no coat to shield the blow—
no mittens for his fingers—
no boots to keep out snow.

The wolf made it seem so perfect—
sliced hot bread, warm apple pies
enjoyed on a summer's day—
he truly was the prince of lies.

...GROWL-L-L-L.....

...OW-OOH...

...HOWL-L-L-OOO...

Gingerboy could hear them howling;
he could tell the wolves were near.
He knew he must keep running
or be frozen by his fear.

Suddenly, across the distance
he heard a tooting train—
like the gift his Papa gave him—
could it take him home again?

...TOOT-TOOT.....

...TOOT-TOOT.....

Gingerboy was running faster,
tears now pouring down his face.
Then he saw the big steam engine.
If he could get there, he'd be safe.

He could hear the wolves were closer.
His every breath now hard to find.
With gnashing teeth they lunged at him.
He was running out of time.

Gingerboy could go no further;
he fell helpless to the ground.
All hope inside had left him,
then he heard a thunderous sound.

The train's Conductor spoke with force,
his voice was loud and clear.
"Be gone, evil intruders,
for you have no power here."

The Conductor looked out; his eyes fixed on one wolf.
That wolf sensed the forbidding stare.
Then realized he'd met the Conductor before,
and felt a terror that he could not bear.

The large wolf then gave the orders
and the wolves all fled in pain.
Feeling safe, Gingerboy jumped up
and felt a joy words couldn't explain.

Oh NO!

I know that voice!

RUN!!

With the Conductor's arms wide open, Gingerboy made a running leap. He embraced his new found friend and, with relief, began to weep.

You're safe here, Gingerboy!

29

CHAPTER 3

"I have no ticket," Gingerboy said between sobs.
The Conductor smiled. "Your ticket is free.
I saved you a seat and it's right over here.
You get to sit right next to me."

Excited, Gingerboy turned 'round to look.
There it was, a nice seat all his own.
"Thank you," he said and gave a big smile.
It felt good to not be so alone.

Clearing his throat, the Conductor looked on,
his booming voice taking command.
"Welcome, all children, to the Christmas Express!
You've entered a magical land."

"We are all on a mission.
We'll travel quite far,
from our snowy train station
to Bethlehem's star."

"The train will go fast,
to view that star in the sky.
Where the train cannot go
we will all simply fly."

"You see, Christmas is coming,
no time to delay.
This star guides a lost world
to the babe born to save."

"And now we are ready to start on this trip.
Make sure all your coats are buttoned and zipped.
The warm air will come as we move ever closer,
but for now the cold holds its grip."

The Conductor pulled a package from under his seat.
He had a very special surprise.
A fluffy down coat as white as new snow,
and it was just exactly his size.

Gingerboy zipped the coat.
He felt warm deep inside
and knew he was safe.
All the chill was outside.

clickety-clack...

clickety-clack...

clickety-clack...

The train whistle blew, the wheels creaked to start;
the adventure was finally here.
The *"clickety-clack"* of the train's railroad tracks
was a lullaby to Gingerboy's ears.

Gingerboy found himself falling asleep
when he was startled by a poke in his side.
Standing before him was a stout little boy,
not as tall as his body was wide.

His face was as round as his two chubby cheeks.
His cheeks the same size as his ears.
His mouth was wide, too, but his nose much too small.
There were times it almost disappeared.

What are you?

"What have we here?" he announced to the crowd.
"It looks like a stale gingersnap!
I'm feeling real hungry, think I'll take a bite.
I'll just make him my afternoon snack."

Gingerboy felt as trapped as he'd been by the wolves, gripped with fear from his head to his toes.
"What, no reply from this icing-drawn mouth?
Time to turn you to raw cookie dough!"

The boy started to laugh, quite amused with himself.
Gingerboy cringed at this boy so mean.
The Conductor could tell what Gingerboy needed most
was a rescue from this scary scene.

The very next moment the brakes gave a squeal.
The Conductor suddenly stopped the train.
Swiftly, he stepped between the two boys,
the anger on his face very plain.

"There is no room on this ride," the Conductor said firmly,
"for actions that bring others pain.
These tracks will guide all to a place of great love.
We are blessed to be on such a train."

The Conductor watched the boy for signs of regret.
With crossed arms, Billy tried to act strong,
but his trembling chin gave it all away.
He felt shame for what he'd done wrong.

The boy turned away, slowly walked to his seat.
It was faint, but they all heard him cry.
Gingerboy then peered into the Conductor's face
and could see there was pain in his eyes.

sniff. . .

sniff. . .

Billy stopped his crying as the Conductor drew near.
A tiny sniffle was the only trace.
His head was tucked tightly underneath his zipped coat,
compassion softened the Conductor's face.

The Conductor leaned down to talk to the boy.
He spoke words both gentle and kind.
"I'm not your accuser, I've come here to help—
to comfort and to soothe your mind."

Billy then peeked outside of his coat,
his face was as red as his eyes.
"I know what I did was not the right thing.
I do wrong no matter how hard I try."

The train was so quiet Gingerboy heard each word.
He understood all that Billy had said.
He had the same choice when he woke up today,
but he did what he wanted instead.

The Conductor and Billy walked toward Gingerboy;
all the children entranced by the scene.
"Forgive me," he said softly to Gingerboy.
"I'm sorry to treat you so mean."

He didn't want to forgive what Billy had done;
he turned his body the other way.
The Conductor knelt down beside Gingerboy.
He knew just what he needed to say.

"Have you ever done something that hurt someone else,
and you knew it was the wrong thing to do?
If you asked forgiveness for the wrong you had done,
wouldn't you want to be forgiven too?"

Gingerboy felt a knot that seemed stuck in his throat.
He shook as he turned Billy's way.
"I'm angry at you," Gingerboy shouted out.
"What you did to me wasn't okay."

"I want to stay angry; I want to stay mad.
I know that way you will hurt, too.
But if I don't forgive what you did today,
I'm doing the same thing to you."

At the same time, they both agreed to forgive;
the train car of children let out a large cheer.
Both boys laughed out loud and then shared a hug,
and the anger and the hurt disappeared.

With the children applauding, the Conductor's voice raised.
"Children, please do hear what I say.
Forgiveness is the magic that heals broken hearts
and why Jesus was born Christmas day."

"This moment of joy that we all share together
is a glimpse of what God has prepared.
Anger and hurt separate us from God.
We pull away and feel empty and scared."

"He sent His son, Jesus, to carry the pain
that stood in the way of God's love.
If we ask forgiveness through Jesus today,
be prepared for a heavenly hug."

CHAPTER 4

The children began to sing old Christmas carols
with a happiness that made them sound new.
Billy took a seat beside his new friend
and decided that he would sing, too.

Gingerboy tried to sing, but only one thing mattered,
that this train go much faster than fast.
He must find this baby who had saved all the world,
and who might bring him to Papa at last.

The wheels began turning as the train gave a toot;
the train ride again had begun.
The wheels keeping time to a slow clicking beat,
while Gingerboy sang, "Here I come!"

The train lurched ahead, passing cities and towns;
wreaths hung from doorways and lights on each side.
Gingerboy saw a snowman waving hello
and wished he could join in the ride.

The train then moved faster,
rounding hillsides of snow.
Children making their snowmen
gave shouts from below.

Each new town they passed had a tree on display,
with bright lights leading up to the star.
But the nativity scene at the front of the church,
Gingerboy found most lovely by far.

The journey grew longer, riders drifted to sleep.
Even Billy became sleepy-eyed.
He chose as his pillow his friend's nearby shoulder
and began snoring his own lullaby.

Gingerboy wished he could gaze at the sights,
but he could not budge an inch on this ride.
As Billy's pillow, he was one trapped sardine
and losing feeling on his left side.

The train picked up speed; the wheels leaving the ground,
in a moment they were high in the sky.
The warm breeze sparked excitement for Gingerboy.
Could his Papa be very close by?

The Conductor leaned forward, his eyes searched the sky,
his hand pointed to a star shining bright.
Now determined, Gingerboy wriggled free
and nudged his friend. "Billy, look at this night!"

Looking down at the world, Gingerboy was amazed.
In the distance, lay a vast desert land.
In place of white pines, palm trees dotted the way
and three men riding fast in the sand.

Billy looked at the sky. Not content with his view, he pushed Gingerboy off to the side.
He quickly said, "Sorry," to his new best friend.
"Gingerboy, I just love this sky ride!"

The lights seemed to move now and even to sing.
"Who are they?" the boys asked. "They seem to have wings."
The Conductor spoke; he seemed almost to pray.
"They are angels who sing for a King."

The weather now warm, the children threw off their coats;
they had an appointment to keep.
A brand new excitement filled each waiting heart.
They were near where the babe lay asleep.

HOORAY!

YEA!

We're here!

Suddenly, pain touched Gingerboy's heart;
he bowed his head and he started to cry.
He missed his dear Papa, it hurt to be apart.
The Conductor took a place by his side.

"What's wrong, Gingerboy? You seem very sad.
Is there something that you'd like to say?"
"I want to be close to my Papa, but a wall gets in the way.
I don't know how to fix it. Could you help it go away?"

"The pain you now feel Jesus Christ understands.
As His son, He loves your Papa, too.
When He came to the earth, He left His Father's home,
because of how much He loved you."

I miss my Papa.

"He has come to fix it.
He's your Savior and your friend.
Ask Jesus into your heart
and you'll be close once again."

Gingerboy could now see he would only find hurt
if his Father and he were apart.
Jesus came to the world on that first Christmas day
to provide the way back to His heart.

The train made a sharp turn then stopped in mid-air.
Another turn—it descended down quick.
Gingerboy's tummy was still in the sky
when the train touched the tracks, "clickety-click."

The train now stopped; Gingerboy was aware
they had finally reached the magical place.
He felt very nervous at what would come next,
but needed to see Jesus' face.

Shepherds gathered 'round the sleeping babe,
His mother and father stood awed.
There in the manger lay their firstborn child,
Baby Jesus, the true Son of God.

"Take my hand, Gingerboy, follow me to the child.
Know the love that He has just for you."
Gingerboy took his hand with one more thought,
"Can Billy come and be with us too?"

"Billy is special," the Conductor affirmed.
"It's important that Billy come, too.
You're all very special, so you all must see Jesus
because He loves each one of you."

He called the waiting children to step off the train
and follow him to this holy place.
No one said a word as he guided each step
for they saw a shining light on his face.

As they came before the manger,
each child made not a sound.
They knew Jesus was their King.
Every knee fell to the ground.

The halo of light glowing over Jesus' head
made His face seem to shine brighter now.
There was no look of judgment at all in His eyes,
a King that demanded no bow.

Gingerboy looked at Jesus and he knew he was loved,
more precious than each star in the sky.
Gingerboy felt his guilt suddenly slip away
and all he could do was to cry.

Gingerboy felt a hand on his shoulder.
The Conductor bowed his head to pray.
Gingerboy somehow knew his faithful guide
would give him the words to say.

"Forgive all my wrongs, my dear Lord and my friend.
Come into my heart, and my Savior you'll be.
I've hurt you the most, still your love never ends.
I will serve you and love you for all eternity."

Amen.

Gingerboy raised his head, wiped the tears from his face.
Angels resounded, singing out songs of praise.
Looking at Baby Jesus, he could see his Father's face.
All of Heaven rejoiced—Gingerboy had been saved!

Gingerboy understood Jesus Christ was the bridge
that led Papa and he back together.
The wall Gingerboy built was now torn away,
and they'd be close now and forever.

Papa?

Gingerboy turned to look high in the clouds.
"I love you, Papa," he cried.
He felt that Papa was now everywhere
and yet still close by his side.

"I dearly love you," his Papa whispered.
"And I've missed my Gingerboy, too.
The victory over evil now has been won
and I will always be close to you."

Gingerboy's heart was bursting with love.
Billy grabbed his hands, jumping for joy.
"I know Jesus loves me," Billy proclaimed.
"Your Father is my Father, Gingerboy."

The Conductor hugged them both to show he loved them, too.
He rejoiced that evil had been erased.
There were children all around giving glory to God,
and a reflection of Heaven on each face.

The angels sang songs of praise and of glory
for evil's power had now been destroyed,
and every child who'd received Jesus' love
would have a father, just like Gingerboy.

Gingerboy looked around at the joyous scene.
As he sang, his heart seemed to soar.
"I love you, Papa," he whispered, softly.
Papa whispered back, "But I love you more."

Gingerboy knew that would always be true.

"But I love you more."

55

About the Author...

Author Joanne Kimberly spent the first eighteen years of her life living in the small town of Hollis, NH. She received her BA in Theatre, English and Secondary Education from the University of New Hampshire. In 1977, she married her husband, David, and they continue to share a fulfilling life in their call to ministry together.

Joanne has taught music and reading at the elementary level, as well as advanced high school English and Theatre. She has served as a high school Drama Department Director and directed numerous middle school, junior high, and high school theatre productions. In addition, she has written and directed five full-length Christian musicals, skits, and puppet shows at the churches she and her husband have been called to serve.

Joanne has satisfied reading endorsement requirements and received secondary Reading Endorsement Certification. As a reading specialist at a local elementary school, she was able to raise children's reading skills, vocabulary, and comprehension up to as much as three grade levels. She has written "Gingerboy's Search for Christmas" for parents and grandparents to read to their children at bed time, to help develop that special bond, and to contribute to children's cognitive development through the message, poetry, and pictures of the story.

As your child follows Gingerboy on his quest to find his Papa, it is her hope that children and adults both will be reminded of how much our Heavenly Father loves us all.

Joanne Kimberly
joanne@happyplacebooks.com

Thank you for joining me on my Christmas adventure! Be sure to visit my website to see where I'll be next! I'd love to hear from you, so write me an email soon, ok? Until then, listen to your parents, say your prayers, be good, and have fun!

gingerboy@happyplacebooks.com

www.happyplacebooks.com

facebook.com/happyplacebooks

Gingerboy

A unique feature of this children's story is that it is written in four separate chapters. It is enjoyed most by children ages 5-10.

We suggest:

- For children ages 5-7, read each chapter in four different readings at bed time.

- For children ages 8-10, encourage them to read it on their own, perhaps making it their first chapter book!

- Children younger than 5 enjoy the book, too, but you may wish to talk through the story through the pictures.

Love

Integrity

Faith

Excellence

.......so that all children might know their Father

DOING THE MOST GOOD

Praying God's blessings on your family this Christmas!

Printed in the USA
FMT401.084015061117

9 780990 489344